Do not separate me O Lord from the chosen, from the joy, from the light and the splendor.
Jewish Sabbath prayer

Published by Dial Books for Young Readers · A Division of Penguin Books USA Inc.
375 Hudson Street · New York, New York 10014

Text copyright © 1994 by Maxine Rose Schur · Pictures copyright © 1994 by Brian Pinkney
All rights reserved · Designed by Nancy R. Leo
Printed in the U.S.A.
First Edition
1 2 3 4 5 6 7 8 9 10

Library of Congress Cataloging-in-Publication Data
Schur, Maxine. Day of delight : a Jewish Sabbath in Ethiopia /
by Maxine Rose Schur ; pictures by Brian Pinkney.
p. cm.
Summary: Depicts a young Ethiopian Jewish boy and his family, including their typical
daily routine followed by preparation for and celebration of the Sabbath.
ISBN 0-8037-1413-0 (trade).—ISBN 0-8037-1414-9 (library ed.)
[1. Jews—Ethiopia—Fiction.   2. Sabbath—Fiction.
3. Ethiopia—Social life and customs—Fiction.]   I. Pinkney, J. Brian, ill.   II. Title.
PZ7.S3964Day 1994   [Fic]—dc20   93-31451   CIP   AC

*The full-color artwork was prepared using scratchboard, a technique that
requires a white board covered with black ink. The ink is then
scraped off with a sharp tool to reveal the white, which is
painted over with oil pastels, oil paints, and gouache.*

DAY OF DELIGHT

A · JEWISH · SABBATH · IN · ETHIOPIA

Maxine Rose Schur · *pictures by* Brian Pinkney

Dial Books for Young Readers

New York

Well before the woodcock calls, when morning still looks like night, my mother rises. Moving silently over the earth floor, she lifts the bamboo pipe from the wall and kneels with it over the hearth. Again and again she blows through the pipe. Again and again, until at last her breath rekindles yesterday's embers.

As the fire grows, my mother mixes *teff* flour with water and pours it on the iron griddle. Now our *injara*, our bread pancakes, are sizzling. We throw off our sheepskin covers and dress in our long *shammas*. Father pours water from the gourd onto our outstretched hands. Around the *massob*, our table made of woven reeds, we eat our pancakes, washing them down with strong coffee.

Suddenly we hear it! The clang of the iron gong, the boom of the big drums. My little brother, Simcha, runs to the door to watch. The elders are moving through the village, reminding us that Sabbath, the Day of Delight, begins at sundown.

Father rises, pours sesame oil into the lantern, and gathers his blacksmithing tools. "Come, Menelik," he says to me. "We have much work, and because of the Sabbath, only a half day to do it."

My mother hands me a bag of roasted chick-peas for our lunch. When I follow my father out of the hut, Simcha begs to come along.

"Our work is not for little ones," Father tells him gently.

Simcha cries, knowing he must stay home to study letters, gather kindling, and shoo stray chickens out the door.

In front of his hut, not far from our own, Uncle Baruch is fanning the fire with the goatskin bellows. Today we will make sickles for cutting down the teff grass. Sickles to sell so we can buy meat, coffee, and salt. My father fits a piece of scrap iron into the tongs and plunges it into the fire. Just before it melts, when it is sun-colored, he pulls it out and rests it on the anvil. With one hand he holds the tongs and with the other he taps his hammer on the hot iron, showing the exact spot where Uncle Baruch must let fall the heavy sledge. CLANG!

Tap...Tap...CLANG! Our metal music rings through our mountain village and echoes across the dark valleys.

The charcoal fire reaches higher. With the long metal poker I push the coals together until they are piled up like a little hill. It is my job to keep the flames big. And though my eyes are filled with smoke, I am happy, for my father promised me that later he will let me take the iron from the fire. All by myself.

By the time the morning sun lights the mountaintops, the rest of the villagers are working. As I tend the fire, I see my mother in front of our hut sitting with the other potter women. Her hands fly like two brown swallows. First she pulls and pinches the red clay until it is soft and pliant. Then she rolls out the long, skinny snakes that she coils around and around to shape a tall jug. Later she will decorate it with juniper leaves, pigeon feathers, and glass beads.

Today she has much to do. Besides making jugs, she must sweep the hut with the horsehair broom, prepare *wat*, our peppery chicken stew, and bake *dabo*, our white Sabbath bread. Simcha kneels in the dirt beside her, scratching alphabet letters with a sycamore twig.

Outside his hut Old Uri sits in a hole weaving. His great high loom is attached to his big toes by strings. His toes are his treadle and as he moves them up and down, the strings lift the wooden slat that makes the threads weave together. A few feet away Uri's wife cleans and spins the raw cotton. They do not speak to each other. Uri must concentrate—he cannot even shoo flies away! If his cloth starts to pucker, he will have to undo the threads and start again.

Old Uri's toes move up and down, hour after hour after hour. In two weeks he will have turned the wild mountain cotton into a milky white shamma to sell at the market.

As I tend the fire, I look toward the hills. I see our men work the soil. They are sharecroppers, farmers who plow the damp dark land they do not own.

I can see Reuben moving slowly, stumbling behind two humpnecked oxen. His long iron plow opens the earth, readying it to receive seeds of teff, the grain we use to make our bread.

Our people depend on a good crop, and every year we wonder: Will the teff grass grow tall and green, bringing enough money at the market to buy meat? Will there be enough rain to start new life within the seeds at all? I am only ten, but I can remember the year when the sky gave no rain at all. I remember how the gray locusts came covering the fields like a great dirty shamma, destroying the crops within hours.

Birds too are trouble. They love to eat the newly planted seeds. But Reuben and the other farmers have planned well. They have built wooden platforms where their sons, armed with slingshots, defend the precious seeds from hungry birds.

At the close edge of these fields the branches of the sycamore tree dance up and down. At first I see no one, but then I spot my friends Isaac and Josef at the top of the tree. Those two are the best climbers in the village; surefooted as mountain goats. I've no time to watch them now, yet I know just what they're doing. They are removing the honey from the beehive baskets. The hanging baskets swarm with angry bees, but my friends have a clever trick. They hit the sides of the baskets softly with sticks, making a sound like slow Sabbath drums. The rhythmic beat calms the bees so Isaac and Josef can open the baskets and safely remove the honeycomb. From this the grown-ups will make sweet beer, and as a treat, give us small golden pieces to crunch.

Throughout the village there is a sound like soldiers marching. The grinding women are banging the big wooden pestles into the stone mortars. Every day they crush barley, maize, and teff grass to make flour. And every day as she works, Widow Debra complains. "Aye!" she always cries. "My shoulders are sore, my neck is stiff, my hands hurt!"

On the Sabbath she will drink bark tea and feel much better. But today she must bang the pestle.

Girls of the village also work hard. Each day I see them run back and forth to the river for water, collect cow dung for fuel, and carry roasted chick-peas to the men in the fields. As I pump the bellows to fan the flame, a girl with a baby on her back drives the cows to the high sod grass. At first the cows file past us like obedient children. But suddenly they stray toward our fire. I grab the iron poker to shoo them back and the girl throws pebbles at the cows and shouts, *"Hid! Hid!"*

When the cows have passed and I've made the fire high again, my father turns to me and says, "Now it is your turn to take the iron from the fire."

I say nothing so he asks, "Menelik, are you afraid?"

"No," I answer, though my heart is beating fast.

Father hands me the tongs. "Wait for the right moment," he warns.

The iron flames red as the sunrise, then white as the moon. Now...no...no... yellow as the sun. Now! With all my strength I swing the tongs up from the fire and land the sizzling metal right on the anvil.

"Perfect!" says my father.

I smile, for I can already picture a long cool curve of iron—without holes, bends, or cracks.

For many more hours we work in silence. Our arms ache and our eyes water from the smoke. Our shammas darken with the soot that flies up from the burning coals.

When the sun sits high in the sky and the air hangs still, we stop. Workday tools are put away. The coal fire is doused. The looms lie silent. The cattle are left to graze. Birds fly freely, as slingshots are laid to rest.

It is time to prepare for the Sabbath.

Back at our hut my mother greets us with clean shammas. "I have already bathed," she says. "Now it is your turn."

We take the clean clothes down to the river. Simcha runs in front of us, scaring the chickens. In the reeds of the riverbank we take off our soot-stained shammas. My skin is hot and dry, so I jump right in. Naked in the cool water, we pass around the green soap my mother made from the wild soapwort berries.

"I'm a crocodile!" I shout as I lunge at Simcha's legs. He shrieks with laughter and splashes me all over. While we play, a sunfish swims around our feet.

"Look," Father says at last. "The sun is dipping. We must leave." Walking back to our hut, I can smell the spicy barberry pepper and garlic of our chicken stew.

Sanbat Salaam," Mother greets us. "Peaceful Sabbath!" Father takes her hand in his. Yesterday she said, "The grass roof needs repair." Yesterday Father told her, "We've no money for sandals this year." But the Sabbath is almost here, so they do not speak of workday things.

In these last moments Simcha and I sit in the breeze near the doorway of our hut as the dusk slowly absorbs the world's colors. No wheel is spun. No water is drawn. No fire is lit. No drum is beaten. No gong is sounded. We can hear our cattle moo in the twilight. We can hear a hyena cry in the hills. We can hear the dry thornbush creak in the wind. Overhead the darkening sky reveals the stars. Now all Africa seems at rest.

The Sabbath is come.

We share our meal in the dim moonlight that shines through the open doorway. We are very hungry but make ourselves eat slowly, tearing off chunks of spongy injara and topping them with delicious mouthfuls of hot chicken stew. "Do crocodiles have Sabbath too?" Simcha suddenly asks, his cheeks round with the food he is chewing.

We all laugh. "No, little one," Mother says. "To a crocodile each day in the river is like every other. But we have one day in the week for remembering God's goodness through play, rest, and prayer."

"And good food!" Simcha adds.

"Yes, and good food." Mother smiles, wiping his mouth.

Before going to bed we sing a Sabbath tune. The familiar melody wraps around us like a soft old blanket. Inside our hut we are happy. And outside the night is still. It's at this time I feel my high mountain village must lie on the very route to heaven.

The next morning my whole village makes a procession uphill to the *mequrab*, our synagogue. We carry pitchers of sweet honey beer and coffee, jars of yogurt, and baskets of dabo bread. Today our shammas have no clay stains. Today our shammas have no soot marks. On Sabbath our clothes are as white as we can make them and without holes.

With one hand I hold the parasol over my mother's head to protect her from the hot sun, and with the other I hold Simcha's hand so he won't pick up the dusty pebbles he loves to collect.

Inside the mequrab it is dark and cool. Sesame oil lanterns glow like tiny suns, lighting up the cloths draped on each wall. Purple, green, red, and yellow, they ripple in the breeze from the open door and shimmer together like a rainbow. My family squeezes in among the worshippers sitting on the ground. Fresh cut grass, sweet basil, coriander leaves, and spicy fenugreek have been spread over the earth floor. In the morning warmth the perfume of the herbs wraps around us all. We have made our own Garden of Eden.

In his tall white turban the High Priest reads prayers in the ancient language of Ge'ez. Reuben translates them for us into our own language, Amharic. Reuben does not follow an ox today but is the guide of us all.

"*Yatabarak Egziaber Amlak Israel!*" we sing. "Blessed be the Owner of the World, the God-King of Israel!"

"We are blacksmiths, farmers, weavers," the High Priest tells us. "We are potters and grinders. But we are all something else too. We are God's chosen. Today, on the Sabbath, we especially remember this. For today we do not struggle for food. Today we are at peace."

Later, after the service, we will share our food with one another. Then Simcha will run races with other children. I will play ragball with Josef, Yoav, and Isaac. And tomorrow...

Tomorrow we will rise again before the sun and work until it is too dark to continue. The Sabbath day will have ended, yet it will remain in our minds, warming us with its fire. For the Sabbath is the flame, forging us together with the memory and the promise of a Day of Delight.

Author's Note

For more than a thousand years Jews have lived in the high mountains of Ethiopia in Africa. These black Jews are called *Falashas* (strangers) by other Ethiopians, but call themselves *Beta Israel:* "Those of the House of Israel." Well into the twentieth century the Beta Israel were so isolated, they believed themselves to be the only Jews in the world.

Many Ethiopian Jews make their living as blacksmiths. Because of this occupation, they have been feared and despised by their neighbors, for throughout much of Africa it is believed that those who work with metal can change themselves into werewolves.

In the mid-1980's thousands of Ethiopians fled to Sudan to escape the civil war and the resulting famine. Many Ethiopian Jews escaped to Israel, where the majority of them now live.

In Israel the Ethiopian Jews no longer live in their traditional way. This then is the story of one Sabbath day in an Ethiopian Jewish village. But more than that, it is the story of a way of life that is quickly vanishing.

Pronunciation Guide

Amharic: AmHARic
Baruch: BarOOK
dabo: DAHbo
Ge'ez: GeeUZ
Hid! Hid!: Heed! Heed!
injara: inJARah
massob: mahSOBE
Menelik: MENelik
mequrab: mookRAB

Sanbat Salaam: SanBAHT Sahlahm
shamma: shomma
Simcha: SIMka
teff: tef
Uri: YURi
wat: wot
Yatabarak Egziaber Amlak Israel:
  YetaBARahk EgzeeAHber Amlahk EESroel
Yoav: YoAHV

Glossary

anvil: an iron block on which metals are hammered into various shapes

barberry: a sharp-tasting red fruit that grows on a bush

barley: a grain ground into a flour for bread and also used to make beer

bellows: an instrument used to increase the flames of a fire

coriander: a fragrant herb belonging to the parsley family

fenugreek: a spicy herb used as a tea and to flavor food

maize: corn

mortar: a hard bowl in which grains and spices are ground into a powder with a pestle

pestle: a club-shaped tool used to grind substances in a mortar

ragball: a ball made of tightly wound rags

sickle: a tool with a hooklike blade and a short handle used to cut tall grains and grasses

soapwort: a plant with pink flowers whose leaves contain a sap used for cleansing